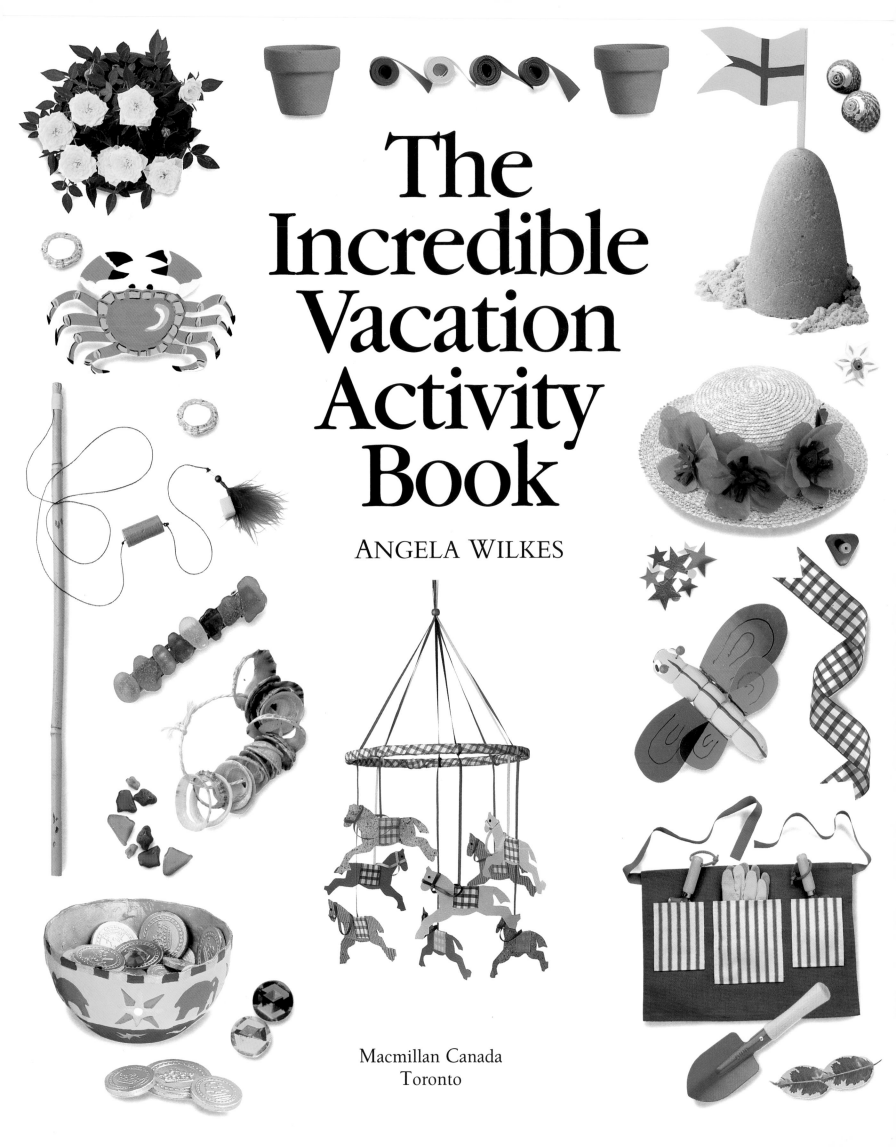

The Incredible Vacation Activity Book

ANGELA WILKES

Macmillan Canada
Toronto

A Dorling Kindersley Book

Art Editor Cheryl Telfer
Editor Victoria Edgley
Photographer Dave King

Managing Editor Jane Yorke
Managing Art Editor Chris Scollen
Production Josie Alabaster
DTP Designer Almudena Díaz
US Editor Camela Decaire

First published in Canada in 1997 by
Macmillan Canada

Canadian Cataloguing in Publication Data

Wilkes, Angela
       Incredible vacation activity book
Includes index.
ISBN 0-7715-7339-1

1. Amusements - Juvenile literature. 2. Handicraft - Juvenile literature.
3. Outdoor recreation - Juvenile literature. 4. Summer - Juvenile. I. Title

GV1203.W545 1997 j790.1'922   C96-931849-9

This book is available at special discounts for bulk purchases by your group or
organization for sales promotions, premiums, fundraisng and seminars.
For details, contact:
Macmillan Canada, Special Sales Department, 29 Birch Avenue, Toronto,
ON M4V 1E2. Tel: 416-963-8830

1 2 3 4 5 DK 01 00 99 98 97

Color reproduction by Bright Arts, Hong Kong
Printed and bound in Italy by A. Montadori Editore, Verona

Picture credits: The Image Bank/ Sumo; 3crb, 43cl, 45tl.

DK would like to thank Alison Dunne for jacket design
and Lissa Martin from World's End Nurseries.
DK would also like to thank the following models
for appearing in this book: Maria Beckworth,
Sarah Bennett, Gina Caffrey, Jay Davis, Candy Day,
Lorna Holmes, Tebedge Ricketts, and Elizabeth Workman.

CONTENTS

OUTDOOR ACTIVITIES

INTRODUCTION

Whether you go away during your vacation or just stay home, this book is full of inspiring ideas for great things to make and do using everyday materials. Before you start, collect some vacation souvenirs and basic equipment. Below you'll see some useful things to save. When you have finished a project, remember to put everything away and clean up any mess you have made.

Things to collect

Spiral-bound notebook

Sketchbook

Leaves

Buttons

Sea glass

Seashells

Paper

Rope

Coins

Map

Ticket

Colored pencils

Disposable pocket camera

String

Keeping record

Notebooks and small sketchbooks are useful for making notes and quick sketches of interesting things that you see. Carry a pocket camera so that you can take photos for souvenirs.

Treasures and souvenirs

Collect as many interesting things as you can find on your vacation. Seashells, pebbles, driftwood, dried leaves, tickets, coins, and maps will form the basis of many of your projects.

Warning symbols

Watch for the red warning signs in the step-by-step instructions of some projects.

The warning symbol

You will see this sign when sharp tools are used. Always ask an adult to help you.

Seeing stars

At the top of each page you will find a star symbol that tells you how long the most difficult project on each page takes.

One star
☆ Project takes an hour or less to complete.

Two stars
☆ Project
☆ takes an afternoon to complete.

Three stars
☆ Project
☆ takes a day
☆ or more to complete.

Colored tape

Tissue paper

Paintbrush

Pencil

Pens

Strong glue

Glue stick

Tape measure

Colored fabric

Scissors   *Craft knife*   *Ruler*   *White glue*

Ribbons

Craft materials

The more craft materials you have, the more choices you will have when making your projects. Collect different colors and types of paper and cardboard. Keep them in a folder so they stay flat. You will also need various kinds of glue, tape, paints, pencils, and pens. Start a bag of fabric scraps and ribbons and put together a small sewing kit with a tape measure, scissors, needles, and pins.

FLUTTERING FLAGS

Even the humblest sand castle can look truly magnificent with its own special flag, so get out your paints and make an array of flags before going to the beach. Try making a colorful pennant to hang at the beach or in your yard.

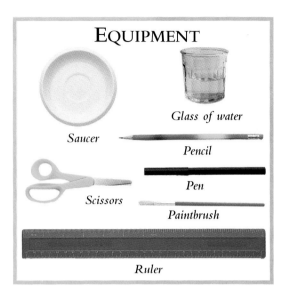
You will need

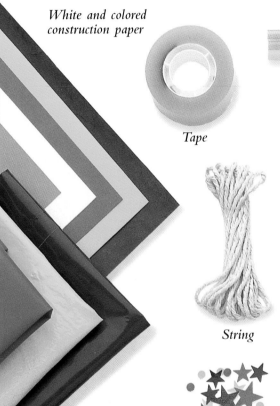

White and colored construction paper

Tape

Plastic drinking straws and swizzle sticks

String

Colored plastic bags

Star and spot stickers

Glue stick

Poster paints   *Strong glue*

Making a pennant

1 Using a pen and ruler, draw lots of triangles the same size on different-colored pieces of plastic. Then carefully cut out the triangles.

2 Fold the top of each triangle over a long piece of string and tape it in place. Space the triangles out along the string.

Making castle flags

1 Draw different-shaped flags on thick paper and cut them out. Paint designs on each one and stick stars or spots on some of the flags.

2 Cut out triangular-shaped flags and fold them several times. Then glue the back edge of each flag to a plastic drinking straw or swizzle stick.

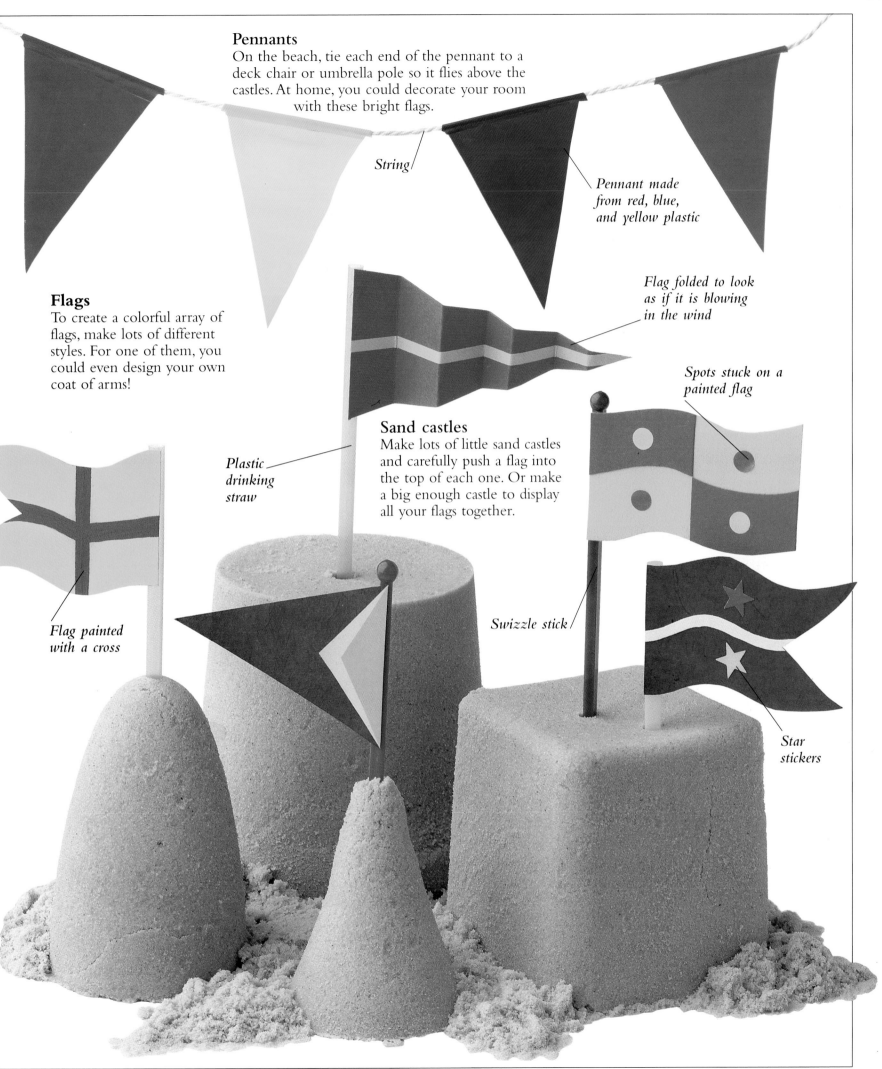

Pennants
On the beach, tie each end of the pennant to a deck chair or umbrella pole so it flies above the castles. At home, you could decorate your room with these bright flags.

String

Pennant made from red, blue, and yellow plastic

Flags
To create a colorful array of flags, make lots of different styles. For one of them, you could even design your own coat of arms!

Flag folded to look as if it is blowing in the wind

Spots stuck on a painted flag

Plastic drinking straw

Sand castles
Make lots of little sand castles and carefully push a flag into the top of each one. Or make a big enough castle to display all your flags together.

Flag painted with a cross

Swizzle stick

Star stickers

GOING FISHING

Here you can find out how to make a simple fishing rod and drop net for your fishing expeditions. Use the rod to catch fish from a riverbank or from a pier. A drop net is good for catching crabs and other small shellfish from tide pools.

You will need

For the rod

Cork

Bamboo stake 6.5 ft (2 m) long

Colored tape

For the drop net

Cubes of bread and cheese for bait

Embroidery rings 14 in (35 cm) across

10 ft (3 m) thick thread or nylon fishing line

Enamel paint

For a lure

13 ft (4 m) thick cord

Thread

Bead   *Paper clip*

Stone

Thread

Colored feathers

20 in x 40 in (50 cm x 100 cm) fine net or mesh

EQUIPMENT

Darning needle

Scissors   *Tape measure*

Needle

Paintbrush

Pins

Making the drop net

1 Fold the net 20 x 20 in (50 x 50 cm). Pin along two sides, leaving one side open. Sew★ the pinned sides about .5 in (1.5 cm) in from the edge.

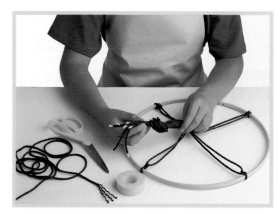

2 To make a handle, cut four pieces of cord each 3 ft (1 m) long. Tie them to the outside embroidery ring, then tie the loose ends together.

3 Tie a stone at the bottom of the net. Fold the top of the net over the inside ring and ask an adult to help you fit the other ring over it.

Making the rod

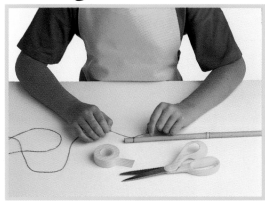

1 Tie one end of the thread to one end of the stake. Wind the thread around the stake several times and hold it in place with colored tape.

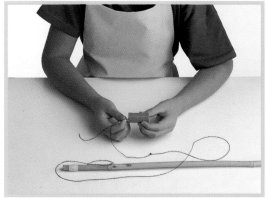

2 Make a hole through a cork with a needle. Paint and let it dry. Knot the thread 3 ft (1 m) from the end, slip on the cork, and tie another knot.

3 Open out a paper clip into a hook and bind feathers to the center with thread. Push a bead on the top end and bend the wire in.

Going for the catch

Hook bait, such as cheese, bread, or bacon rind, on your fishing line, or hang it from the drop net's handle. Now just wait for a catch!

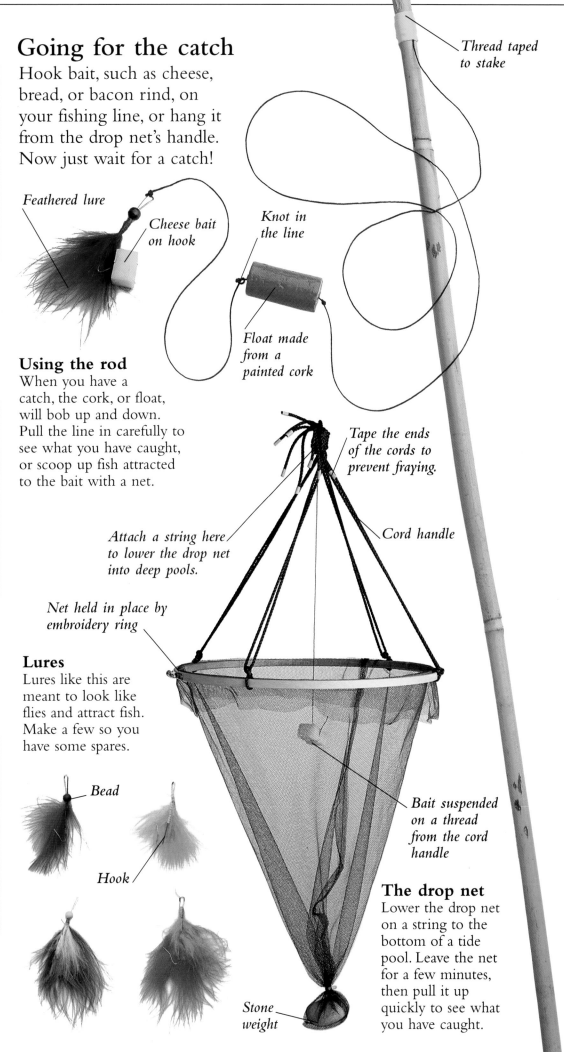

Feathered lure

Cheese bait on hook

Knot in the line

Float made from a painted cork

Thread taped to stake

Using the rod
When you have a catch, the cork, or float, will bob up and down. Pull the line in carefully to see what you have caught, or scoop up fish attracted to the bait with a net.

Attach a string here to lower the drop net into deep pools.

Net held in place by embroidery ring

Tape the ends of the cords to prevent fraying.

Cord handle

Lures
Lures like this are meant to look like flies and attract fish. Make a few so you have some spares.

Bead

Hook

Bait suspended on a thread from the cord handle

Stone weight

The drop net
Lower the drop net on a string to the bottom of a tide pool. Leave the net for a few minutes, then pull it up quickly to see what you have caught.

GARDEN WATCH

To attract wildlife into your yard, set up some mini-habitats. Here and on the next page you can find out how to make a bee and butterfly garden, build a log-pile habitat, set up insect traps, and keep mini-beast records in a nature notebook with a chart. Start the bee and butterfly garden in spring so you can watch it grow and attract insects over the summer months.

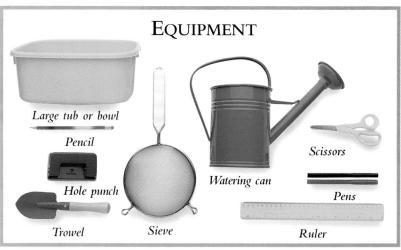

EQUIPMENT

Large tub or bowl

Pencil

Hole punch

Trowel

Sieve

Watering can

Scissors

Pens

Ruler

You will need

For the log-pile habitat

Soil

Bark and twigs

Fern

Primula

Large brick

Logs

For the insect traps

Small tile

Miniature flowerpot

Grapefruit

Potato

Bacon rind and bread

Ivy

For the bee and butterfly garden

Four small stones

Yogurt container

Dry leaves

Lavender

For the chart and notebook

Tape

Strong glue

Thyme

Spiral-bound notebook

Cord

Colored pencils

Bug bottle

Green, white, and yellow poster board

Thin ribbon

Small leaves

Sunflower seeds

Flowerpot and saucer

Log-pile habitat

1 Find a corner of the yard. You could make this in a window box, too. Stack and arrange some logs, bricks, and bark on the soil.

2 Plant the ivy, fern, primula, and any other plants to create a natural environment. Fill in empty areas with dead leaves and small twigs.

3 To make a pitfall trap, scoop out a hole in the ground and sink the yogurt container into it. Drop some bacon rinds into the container as bait.

4 Lay the four stones around the top of the container, as shown. Place a small tile on top of the stones so that it is raised above the rim.

5 To make hideaways for insects and other creepy crawlies, stuff flowerpots with dead leaves. Lay the pots on their sides.

6 For an extra trap, cut a grapefruit in half, scoop out the middle, and put cubes of bread in it. Try it with a potato, too. Place them in the habitat.

Bee and butterfly garden

1 To repot a plant, put some potting soil in the bottom of a new, larger pot. Gently remove the plant and soil from its old pot as shown.

2 Lower the plant into the new flowerpot, then fill the pot with soil. Press the soil down firmly around the plant and water it well.

3 For the sunflowers, fill a pot with soil. Push five sunflower seeds into the soil .25 in (1 cm) deep. Water the soil and do not let it dry out.

NATURE SURVEY

Nature chart

Decorate some poster board and make a chart by drawing grids on paper. Make a hole with the hole punch and attach the grids with cord.

Studying mini-beasts

1 Try sifting some soil and leaves from the log-pile area into a large bowl. How many types of mini-beasts do you find left in the sieve?

2 Put any creatures you find in the bug bottle to study them. Draw them accurately and then put them back where you found them.

Wildlife in the garden

Keep a regular watch on the log-pile habitat and bee and butterfly garden to see how many creatures are attracted to them. Practice making quick sketches of creatures you find. To find out more about the mini-beasts, you could look them up in a reference book.

Nature chart

week 1				
🪲				✓
🐞			✓	
🐌	✓			
🐜		✓		
🪱				
🐌	✓		✓	

Grids

Insect trap chart
Draw the traps at the top of the chart and the creatures you find on the left-hand side. Use the chart to record the creatures you find in the insect traps by checking off the correct box. You could add the time and date that you found the insects, too.

Log-pile habitat
Carefully lift logs and bricks and look under dead leaves to find out which creatures have moved into your log pile. Regulary check the insect traps and make a note of what you find in them. Make sure you release any mini-beasts caught in the traps.

Nature notebook
Make sketches of insects in your notebook. Start with three circles - for the head, thorax, and abdomen. Then add legs, wings or wing cases, antennae, and any special features.

Ivy

Large brick

Head

Abdomen

Garden
mini-beasts

Thorax

Bee and butterfly garden
Plant this garden in spring. Place the
pots in a sunny spot and water them to
keep the soil damp. Butterflies and bees
are attracted to most plants with flowers,
so you could choose other flowering
plants for the garden instead.

Bee

Primula

Butterfly

Thyme

Sunflowers

Lavender

Fern

Twigs

Potato trap

Log

Grapefruit trap

Pitfall trap

Flowerpot
hideaway

13

MINIATURE GARDEN

Here and on the next page you can find out how to create a real miniature garden of your own, complete with its own patio and garden furniture. Below are a selection of some plants you could use, but if you can't find these, use similar plants. For an outdoor garden, the best plants to use are miniatures, with tiny flowers and small leaves.

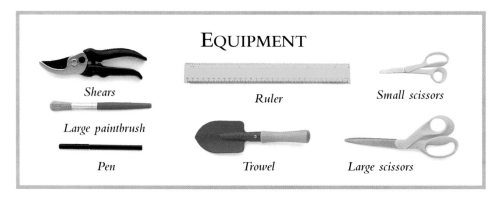

EQUIPMENT

Shears

Large paintbrush

Pen

Ruler

Trowel

Small scissors

Large scissors

You will need

For the garden furniture

For the garden

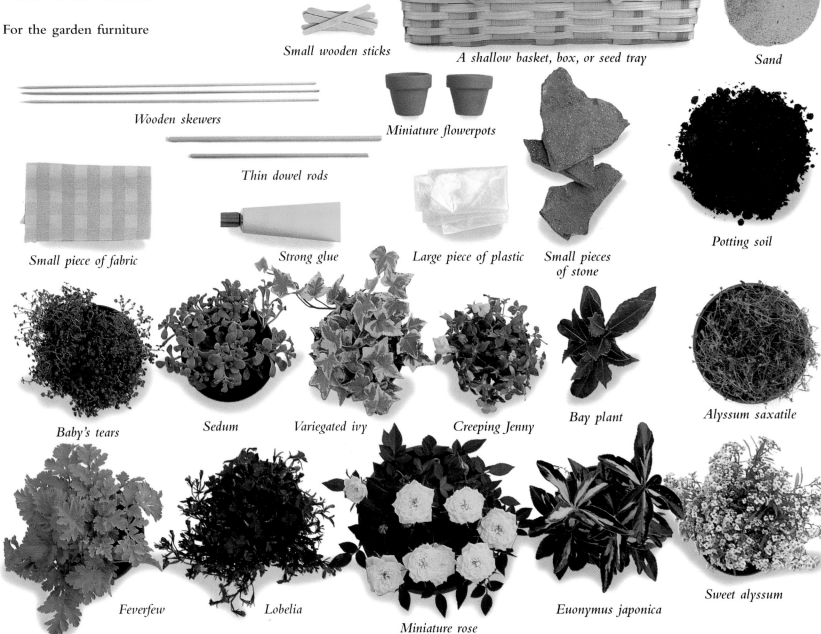

Small wooden sticks

A shallow basket, box, or seed tray

Sand

Wooden skewers

Miniature flowerpots

Potting soil

Thin dowel rods

Small piece of fabric

Strong glue

Large piece of plastic

Small pieces of stone

Baby's tears

Sedum

Variegated ivy

Creeping Jenny

Bay plant

Alyssum saxatile

Feverfew

Lobelia

Miniature rose

Euonymus japonica

Sweet alyssum

Making the deck chair

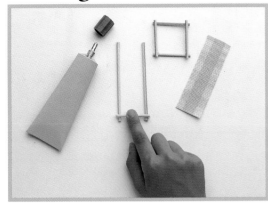

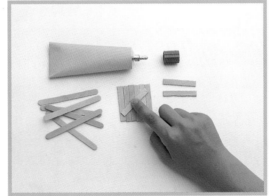

1 Cut★ five 2-in (5-cm) sticks from a wooden skewer. Glue four into a square. Glue the fifth to the end of two 4-in (10-cm) sticks, as shown.

2 Glue the square to the sides of the long sticks to make a deck chair frame. Attach a strip of fabric 1.5 x 4 in (4 x 10 cm) to make a seat.

Making the trellis

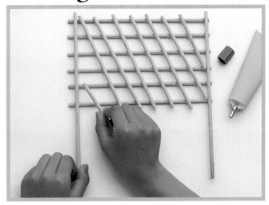

Glue six 8-in (20-cm) dowel rods to two 8.5-in (22-cm) sticks. Cut★ six 5-in (13-cm) and two 3-in (8-cm) sticks. Glue as shown.

Making the pyramid

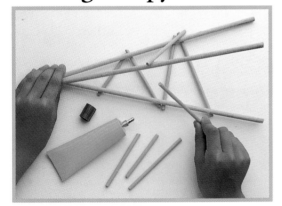

To make a pyramid, join the ends of three 12-in (30-cm) dowel rods. Stick short dowel rod pieces of varying length across them.

Making the table

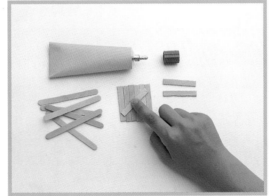

1 Cut★ seven 2.25-in (6-cm) sticks. Put six sticks together for a table top and glue the last stick across them to hold them together.

2 For legs, glue four 2-in (5-cm) dowel rod pieces to each end of two 2-in (5-cm) sticks. Glue the sticks under the table top, as shown.

Making the garden

1 Line the basket with some plastic and cut small holes for drainage. Using the trowel, fill the basket about two-thirds full with potting soil.

2 Now plan out your garden. Leave the plants in their containers and arrange them in the basket to see where they look best.

3 Decide where to position the trellis, path, and patio. Make a patio and path by laying large and small stones on the soil.

A SMALL WORLD
Planting the garden

1 Remove the plants from the pots and plant any tall plants. Put the trellis and pyramid in place. Add ivy by the trellis and a rose in the pyramid.

A secret garden

The finished garden is a real world in miniature, with winding paths and shady spots for tables and deck chairs. Place the garden outside in a bright spot and water it well. It is important to care for your garden and maintain your plants all year round. Trim the plants if they get too overgrown, and snip off any dead leaves or flowers. Keep the soil moist by spraying it with water from a spray bottle.

Feverfew

Steps created by laying stones on top of each other

Lobelia

Snip off any dead flower heads to encourage the plants to keep flowering.

2 To make a lawn, plant creeping, low-growing plants, such as Baby's tears. Carefully press the plants in place.

3 Fill in all the gaps in the garden with small, brightly colored flowering plants. Lobelia and sweet alyssum make good fillers.

4 Sprinkle sand over the patio and paths. Use a wide paintbrush to brush the sand into the cracks between the stones.

5 Add the garden furniture. Fill the miniature flowerpots with small flowers or herb plants and position them in the garden.

Miniature rose
entwined through
pyramid

Ivy woven
through trellis

Miniature
bay plant
in a pot

Patio area

Sedum

Sand brushed
between stones

Path made of
small stones

Cane basket lined
with plastic and
filled with soil

TOP TO TOE

With a little imagination you can transform ordinary straw hats, baseball caps, and canvas sneakers into personalized works of art that are fun to make as well as wear. Gather together colorful beads, buttons, and other odds and ends before you start.

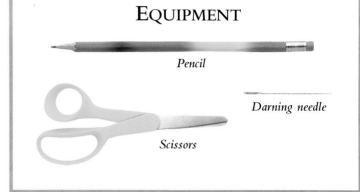

EQUIPMENT

Pencil

Darning needle

Scissors

You will need

For the cap

For the shoes

For the sun hat

Baseball cap

Strong glue

Colored buttons

Washers

Colored beads

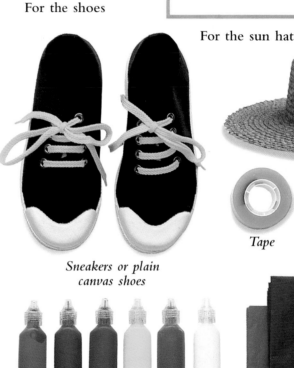

Sneakers or plain canvas shoes

Tubes of all-surface fabric paint★

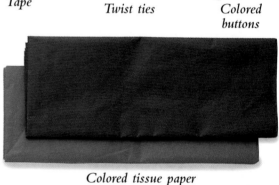

Straw sun hat

Tape

Twist ties

Colored buttons

Colored tissue paper

Straw sun hat

1 Cut large and small flowers out of red and purple tissue paper. Roll up strips of purple tissue. Secure the rolls with tape and snip a fringe.

2 Glue together several flower shapes. Thread a button on a tie and twist the end to secure it. Pull the tie through a purple roll.

3 Push a tie through the center of a flower. Thread the needle with the tie and attach it to the crown of the hat. Bend the tie back to secure it.

Canvas shoes

Remove the laces from the shoes. Paint shapes and pictures on the shoes in one color. Leave to dry. Use another color to fill in the shapes.

Baseball cap

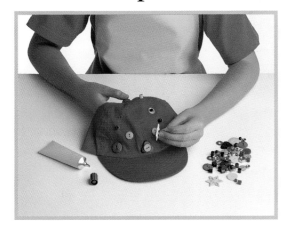

Glue buttons, beads, and washers to the cap in a pattern. Stick smaller buttons and beads on top of larger ones to add more detail.

Stepping out

Copy these decorative ideas or experiment with your own. For example, you could try covering a straw hat or sneakers with buttons and a baseball cap with fabric paints.

Nautical shoes
These canvas shoes have a seaside theme, with pictures of a boat, anchor, and life buoy.

Bright yellow laces add a splash of color.

Wavy waterline

Wavy piece of cord

Buttons attached to the visor

Fish-shaped buttons

Button caps
Use brightly colored beads and buttons in as many different shapes as you can find to decorate your cap and create patterns.

Washer and bead on top of a button

Fringed purple tissue paper with a button in the center

Purple flowers made in the same way as the red flowers

Red flower petals

Floral sun hat
Fasten three large red flowers to the front of the hat, and smaller purple flowers around the crown.

DECORATING T-SHIRTS

You can transform plain T-shirts with amazing designs by painting, printing, stenciling, or tie-dying them. Use white or light-colored T-shirts for the best results and choose fabric paints in strong, contrasting colors. It is a good idea to draw a clear design for each T-shirt before you start. Turn the page to see what great works of art you can produce in an afternoon.

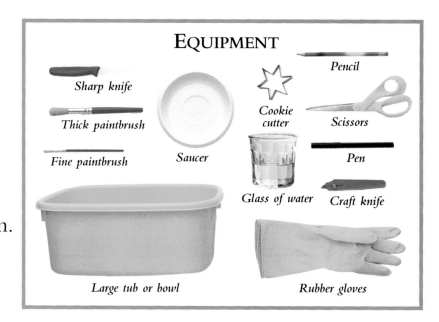

EQUIPMENT

Sharp knife

Thick paintbrush

Fine paintbrush

Saucer

Cookie cutter

Glass of water

Pencil

Scissors

Pen

Craft knife

Large tub or bowl

Rubber gloves

You will need

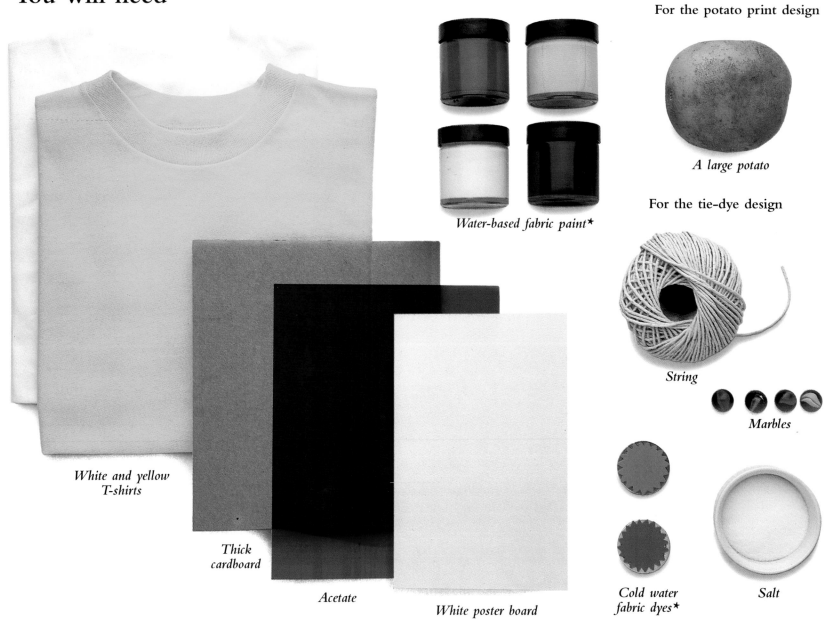

White and yellow
T-shirts

Thick
cardboard

Acetate

White poster board

Water-based fabric paint★

For the potato print design

A large potato

For the tie-dye design

String

Marbles

Cold water
fabric dyes★

Salt

★Available from large department or arts and crafts stores.

Stenciled T-shirt

1 Draw shapes for stencils on the acetate. Lay the acetate on thick cardboard and ask an adult to cut the shapes out with a craft knife.

2 Lay a stencil flat on the T-shirt. Decide which color paint to use, then dab it all over the cutout stencil with a paintbrush.

3 Carefully lift the stencil off the T-shirt so you do not smudge the paint. Continue using other stencils and different colors. Leave to dry.

Hand-painted T-shirt

1 Draw a design on some white poster board to the size you want for your T-shirt. Use a dark pen and keep the design bold and simple.

2 Slip the poster board inside the T-shirt so the design is where you want it. Paint over the outline of the design in a light-colored fabric paint.

3 Paint in the main color of the design and let it dry. Then add the details in other colors, keeping the paint as thick as you can.

Potato print T-shirt

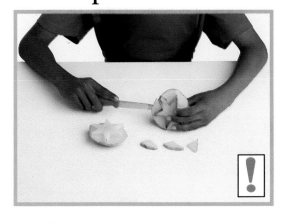

1 Slice a potato in half. Press a star-shaped cookie cutter into each half of the potato. Then carefully cut away the potato around the cutter.

2 Mix some thick paint in a saucer. Cover the potato star with a good coat of paint, then firmly press it down in position on the T-shirt.

3 Lift the potato off carefully. Use the other half of the potato to print another color. Repaint the potatoes each time you use them.

T-SHIRTS ON SHOW

The finished T-shirts are bold and colorful. Let the paint or dye on each T-shirt dry, then ask an adult to help you iron them. You can copy the designs shown here, or try experimenting with pictures and patterns of your own.

Tie-dyed T-shirts

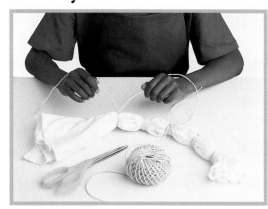

1 To make a stripy T-shirt, roll up a white T-shirt tightly. Tie long pieces of string securely around the T-shirt at 3-in (10-cm) intervals.

2 For a circular design, tie a marble in the middle of the T-shirt's front and in each sleeve. Tie string at 2-in (5-cm) intervals from each marble.

A white T-shirt tie-dyed in red with marbles and string creates a circular effect.

Red and yellow star-shaped potato prints

An all-over design of hand-painted sunflowers

Circular T-shirt

Starry T-shirt

Sunflower T-shirt

3 Wearing rubber gloves, mix the cold water dye in a tub. Follow the instructions on the packet and add the salt. Soak the T-shirt in the dye.

4 After one hour, take the T-shirt out of the dye and wring it out well. Rinse the T-shirt under cold water until the water runs clean.

5 Very carefully cut the string tied around the T-shirt and remove all the ties and marbles. Hang the T-shirt up to dry, then iron it.

Large hand-painted picture

A white T-shirt tie-dyed in blue with string creates these stripes.

Stenciled fish and seashells around the top and bottom

Rooster T-shirt   **Stripy T-shirt**   **Seaside T-shirt**

SUMMER COOLERS

What's better on a hot summer day than a cool, refreshing drink? Here are three tasty recipes for you to try. The sunset punch and fruit cooler can be made in minutes, and both make enough for two people. The fresh lemonade needs to be prepared one day in advance before drinking. This recipe makes enough for four thirsty people.

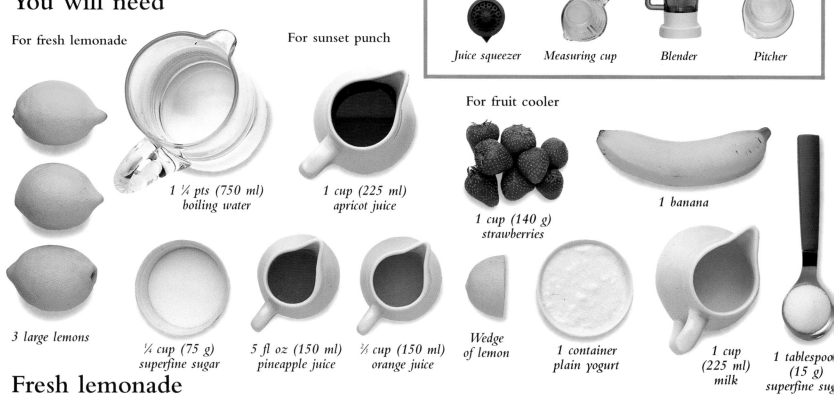

EQUIPMENT

Cutting board

Potato peeler

Sieve

Large spoon

Large bowl

Sharp knife

Juice squeezer

Measuring cup

Blender

Pitcher

You will need

For fresh lemonade

1 ¼ pts (750 ml) boiling water

For sunset punch

1 cup (225 ml) apricot juice

For fruit cooler

1 cup (140 g) strawberries

1 banana

3 large lemons

¼ cup (75 g) superfine sugar

5 fl oz (150 ml) pineapple juice

⅔ cup (150 ml) orange juice

Wedge of lemon

1 container plain yogurt

1 cup (225 ml) milk

1 tablespoon (15 g) superfine sugar

Fresh lemonade

1 Wash the lemons. With the peeler, remove the peel from two lemons into a bowl. Trim off any white pieces of pith you find on the peel.

2 Cut all three lemons in half and squeeze their juice into the bowl. Add the sugar, then carefully stir in the boiling water.

3 Leave the lemonade in a cool place overnight. Then strain the mixture through a sieve into a pitcher, ready to serve.

Fruit cooler

1 Peel the banana. Slice and put it into the blender. Squeeze a little lemon juice on top. Wash the strawberries and chop off the stalks.

2 Put the yogurt into the blender with the bananas, strawberries, milk, and sugar. Blend for about a minute, until frothy. Pour into a glass.

Sunset punch

Pour the orange juice, pineapple juice, and apricot juice into a pitcher and mix them together well with a large spoon. Chill before serving.

Fruity refreshers

Pour the drinks into tall glasses. Add ice cubes made from fruit juice, or try making cubes with pieces of fruit set into them, and serve with sliced fruit and straws.

Sunset punch

Add ice cubes made from cranberry juice for a sunset glow.

Novelty drinking straw

Fresh lemonade

Fruit cooler

Strawberry slotted onto the edge of the glass

Half a strawberry frozen into an ice cube

Cut a slit to the middle of each orange and lemon slice and slot them onto the glass.

ALL IN A POCKET

Here you can find out how to make a cook's apron, a gardener's apron, a tool kit, and an organizer. Copy the patterns at the bottom of the page using the measurements shown. Use a running stitch* to sew the aprons. Turn the page to see the final results.

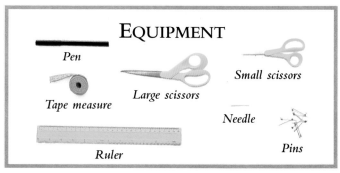

EQUIPMENT

Pen

Tape measure

Large scissors

Small scissors

Needle

Pins

Ruler

You will need

Dowel rods for organizer

Colored curtain fabric

Graph paper

Thread to match your fabric

6.5 ft (2 m) of ribbon for each project

Making the patterns

Copy the apron and pocket patterns below onto graph paper using the measurements shown and cut them out. Adapt the patterns to fit you if they are too big or small. Pin the pattern pieces you need to the fabric, making sure that they are straight. Cut the fabric out, then remove the pattern pieces.

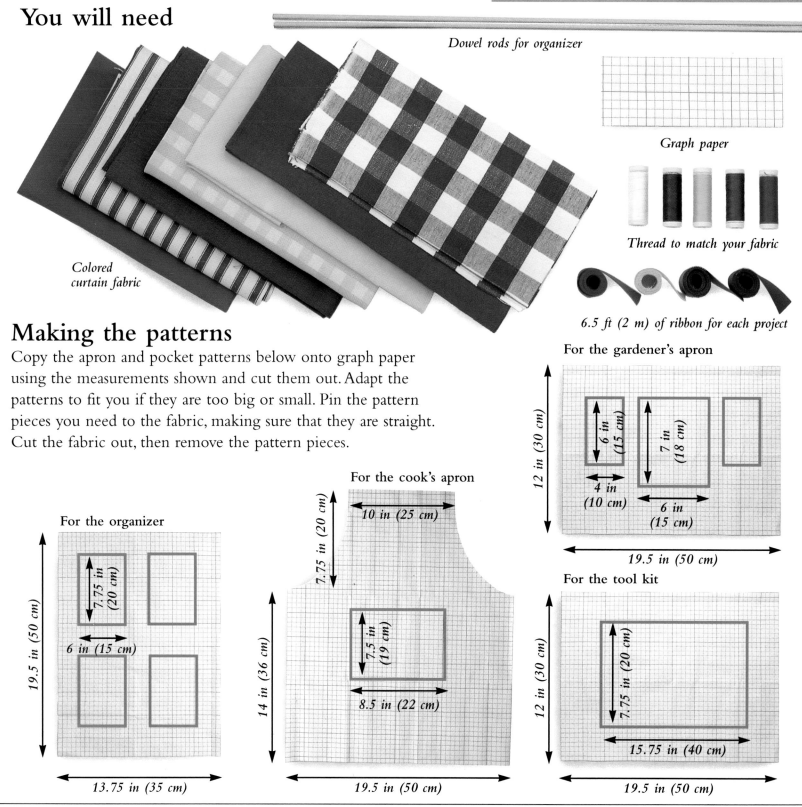

For the gardener's apron

12 in (30 cm)

6 in (15 cm)

7 in (18 cm)

4 in (10 cm)

6 in (15 cm)

19.5 in (50 cm)

For the cook's apron

10 in (25 cm)

7.75 in (20 cm)

7.5 in (19 cm)

8.5 in (22 cm)

14 in (36 cm)

19.5 in (50 cm)

For the organizer

7.75 in (20 cm)

6 in (15 cm)

19.5 in (50 cm)

13.75 in (35 cm)

For the tool kit

12 in (30 cm)

7.75 in (20 cm)

15.75 in (40 cm)

19.5 in (50 cm)

Making the cook's apron

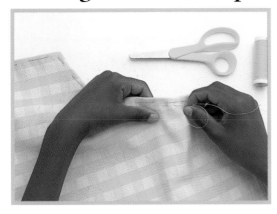

1 To make a neat hem, fold the apron material over .25 in (1 cm) at the edge and fold it again. Tack★ the edge, then sew it in running stitch.

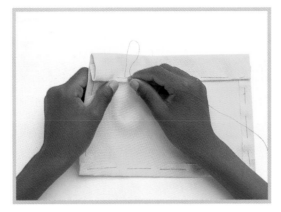

2 Tack a .25-in (1-cm) hem along the sides and bottom of the pocket. Tack and sew a .5-in (1.5-cm) hem at the top edge of the pocket.

3 Pin the pocket to the center of the apron. Tack the pocket in place, then sew it in running stitch along the bottom and sides.

Making the organizer

4 Tack a line across the middle of the pocket to divide it in two. Using the tacking as a guide, sew a straight line across the pocket.

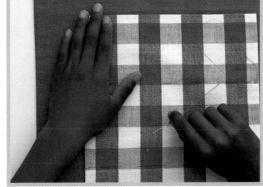

5 Cut a ribbon 22 in (56 cm) for the top and two ribbons 19.5 in (50 cm) for each side. Fold over the ends and sew them to the apron back.

Making the tool kit

1 Tack and sew a .25-in (1-cm) hem on the long sides of the fabric. Tack and sew a .75-in (2 cm) hem at the top and bottom.

2 Make the pockets as in step 2 above. Pin, tack, and sew them on. Cut a ribbon 15.75 in (40 cm) long and sew it to the top of the organizer.

1 Sew the edges of the kit. Tack and sew on the pocket as for the apron. To divide up the pocket, sew two lines 4 in (10 cm) from each side.

2 Cut four 19.5-in (50-cm) lengths of ribbon. Sew two ribbons on the back of the top right corner and the other two to the bottom corner.

★To tack, sew in big stitches using contrasting thread. Remove the tacking stitches when you have done the running stitch.

KITS AND APRONS
Making the gardener's apron

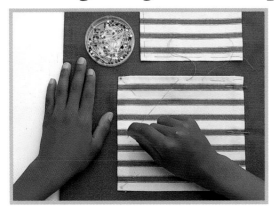

1 Hem the edges of the apron and make the pockets as for the cook's apron. Sew the pockets to the apron 2.75 in (7 cm) from the top edge.

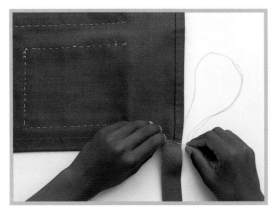

2 Cut two pieces of ribbon 19.5 in (50 cm) long. Turn the edges and sew one ribbon to each top edge of the apron at the back of the fabric.

Finished products

Choose fabrics in bold colors or patterns for the kit and aprons. Checks and stripes look good with plain colors and are easy to sew because you can use them as guidelines for stitching.

Organizer
Hang the organizer on your bedroom wall or above a desk. Use it to hold all your pens and store other odds and ends.

Hang the organizer up by the ribbon loop.

To make the organizer hang correctly, insert the dowel rods into the .75-in (2-cm) hems at the top and bottom.

Individual pockets

Pocket in a contrasting color to checked fabric

Gardener's apron
Tuck your gardening tools, gloves, and packets of seeds away in these practical pockets. Roll up the apron when you have finished using it.

Two smaller pockets on each side of a large pocket

Tool kit

Keep your work area neat by putting your tools, screws, and nails together in the divided pockets of the tool kit. Roll the kit up, starting from the end without the ties. Fasten the kit by tying the four ties at the end around the kit.

Two ties sewn to one side at the top

Two ties sewn at the bottom of the kit

Pocket divided into three by two lines of stitching

Try the apron patterns against you before cutting them out and make them longer or wider if you want.

Tie sewn onto back of apron

Cook's apron

Wear this apron to protect your clothes when you are cooking. Keep useful kitchen tools at hand in the apron pocket.

This pocket is divided in two by a line of stitching.

MARVELOUS MOBILES

When it's raining outside and you are stuck indoors, why not make a fun mobile for your room? Here you can find out how to make three mobiles from poster board, cardboard, or oven-hardening modeling clay, all using the same basic method. Copy the themes we have shown here, or design one of your own.

You will need

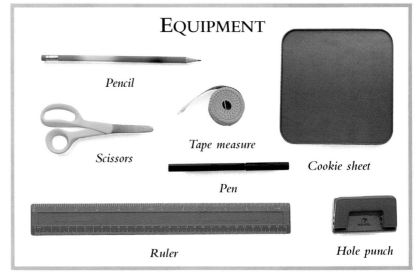

EQUIPMENT

Pencil

Scissors

Tape measure

Cookie sheet

Pen

Ruler

Hole punch

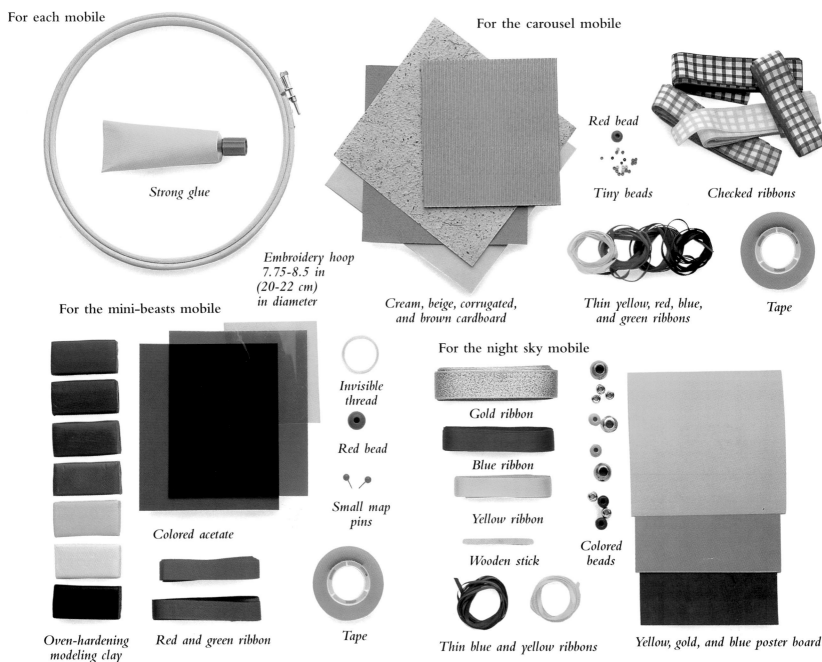

For each mobile

Strong glue

Embroidery hoop 7.75-8.5 in (20-22 cm) in diameter

For the carousel mobile

Red bead

Tiny beads

Checked ribbons

Thin yellow, red, blue, and green ribbons

Tape

Cream, beige, corrugated, and brown cardboard

For the mini-beasts mobile

Invisible thread

Red bead

Small map pins

For the night sky mobile

Gold ribbon

Blue ribbon

Yellow ribbon

Colored beads

Colored acetate

Oven-hardening modeling clay

Red and green ribbon

Tape

Wooden stick

Thin blue and yellow ribbons

Yellow, gold, and blue poster board

Night sky mobile

1 Draw stars and moons on yellow, gold, and blue poster board and cut them out. For the center of the mobile, cut out a big quarter moon.

2 Punch a hole in each shape. Tie a thin ribbon through the hole and thread on a bead. Tie the moon to a wide ribbon 15.75 in (40 cm) long.

3 Cover the embroidery hoop by wrapping blue and gold ribbon around it. Glue the ends of the ribbons in place to secure them.

Mini-beasts mobile

4 Cut four ribbons 12 in (30 cm) long. Glue one end of the ribbons to the hoop. Push the other ends and the moon's ribbon through a big bead.

5 Hold the mobile up to check that it hangs straight. Tie on the other stars and moon, checking that the mobile is still hanging straight.

1 Knead the clay and roll it into balls. Shape characters and leaves with different-colored clay. Use the stick to help model the mini-beasts.

2 Put the mini-beasts on a cookie sheet and harden them in the oven.★ Allow to cool. For some insects, glue on colored acetate wings.

3 Tie thread to each mini-beast and check that it will hang straight. You may need to tie a thread to each end of the mini-beast for balance.

4 Tape ribbons to the hoop, as above. Glue the clay leaves around the hoop for decoration. Hang the mobile up and tie on the mini-beasts.

★Ask an adult to help you harden the clay. Always follow the instructions on the package carefully.

MERRY-GO-ROUND!
Carousel mobile

1 Wrap checked ribbon around the hoop. Cut eight thin ribbons 35 in (90 cm). Tie them to the hoop. Leave 18 in (45 cm) on each side.

2 Draw eight horse shapes on cardboard and cut them out. Glue on the checked-ribbon saddles and the thin ribbon bridles and reins.

3 Thread the eight ribbons through a bead and check that the mobile hangs straight. Tape the other ends of the ribbons to the backs of the horses.

Displaying your mobile
Tie a loop in the ribbons above the bead and ask an adult to help you hang the mobile from the ceiling. Once it is up, you may have to adjust the position of some of the hanging objects so that the mobile balances well. For the best effect, hang the mobile where it will turn slowly in a breeze.

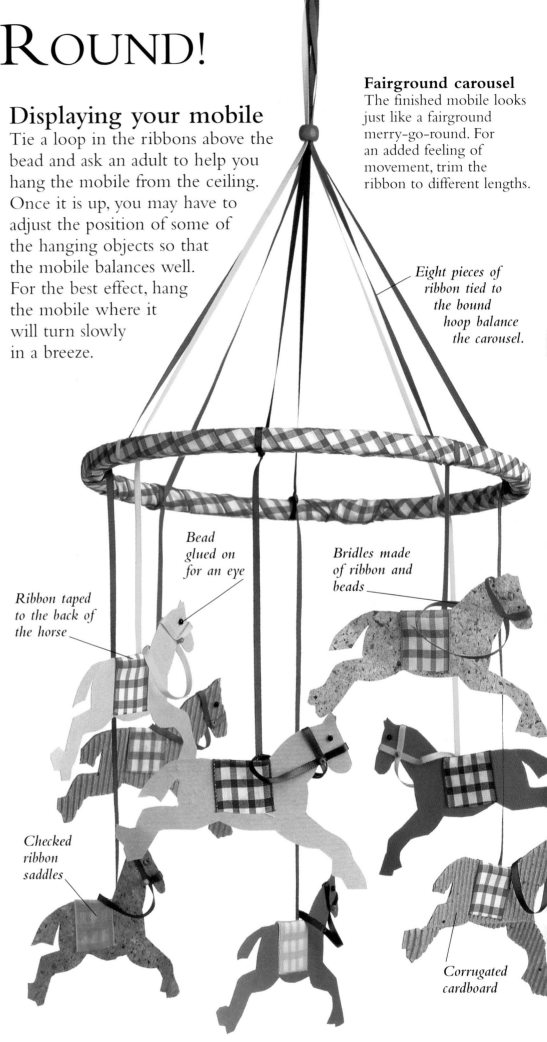

Fairground carousel
The finished mobile looks just like a fairground merry-go-round. For an added feeling of movement, trim the ribbon to different lengths.

Eight pieces of ribbon tied to the bound hoop balance the carousel.

Bead glued on for an eye

Bridles made of ribbon and beads

Ribbon taped to the back of the horse

Checked ribbon saddles

Corrugated cardboard

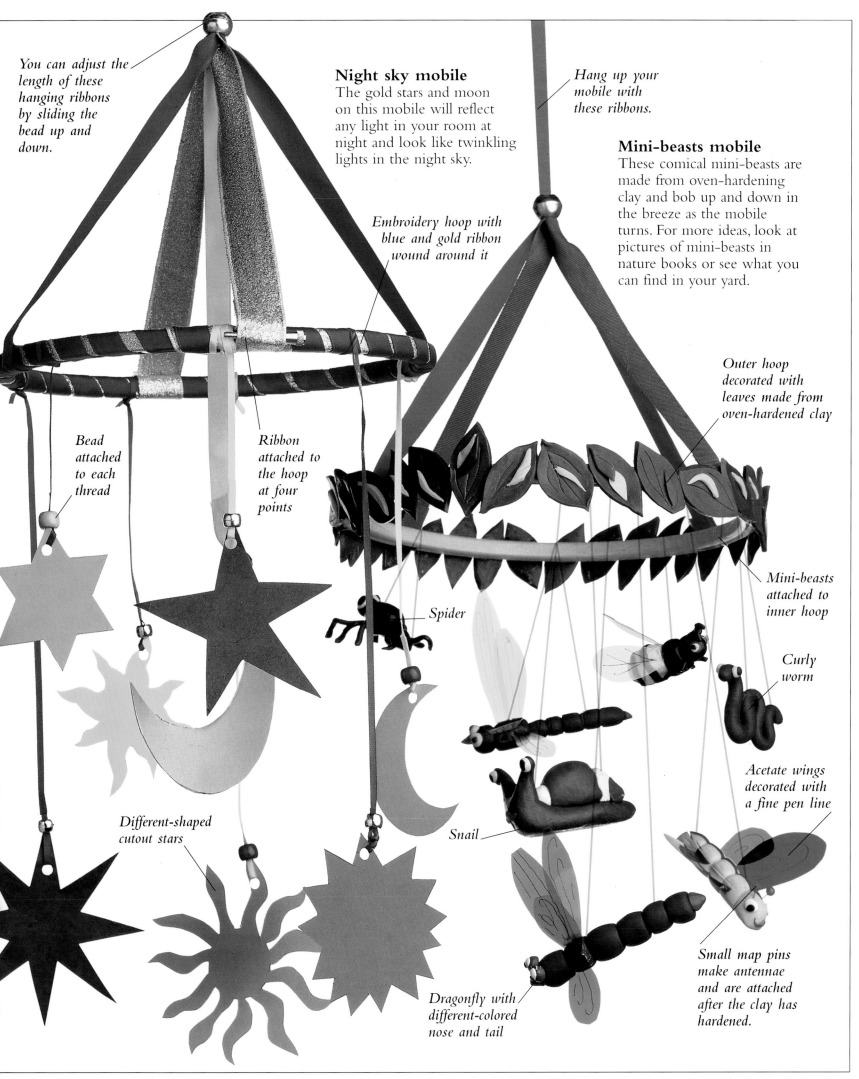

You can adjust the length of these hanging ribbons by sliding the bead up and down.

Night sky mobile
The gold stars and moon on this mobile will reflect any light in your room at night and look like twinkling lights in the night sky.

Hang up your mobile with these ribbons.

Mini-beasts mobile
These comical mini-beasts are made from oven-hardening clay and bob up and down in the breeze as the mobile turns. For more ideas, look at pictures of mini-beasts in nature books or see what you can find in your yard.

Embroidery hoop with blue and gold ribbon wound around it

Outer hoop decorated with leaves made from oven-hardened clay

Bead attached to each thread

Ribbon attached to the hoop at four points

Mini-beasts attached to inner hoop

Spider

Curly worm

Different-shaped cutout stars

Snail

Acetate wings decorated with a fine pen line

Dragonfly with different-colored nose and tail

Small map pins make antennae and are attached after the clay has hardened.

33

UP PERISCOPE!

Here you can see how to make a periscope - an amazing device for seeing things beyond your scope of vision. Periscopes were originally used on submarines to see what was above the surface of the water, but you can use one for spying on friends when they least suspect it. Use it for peering over walls or around corners - it really works!

Making the periscope

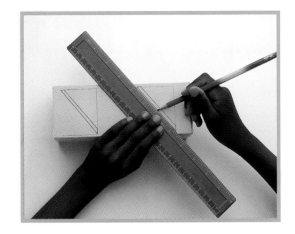

1 Cut off the carton top. Draw two right-angled triangles with 2-in (5-cm) sides on one side. Draw two lines parallel to the diagonal lines.

2 Ask an adult to cut out two slots along the diagonal lines using a craft knife and a ruler. Hold the carton carefully to keep it steady.

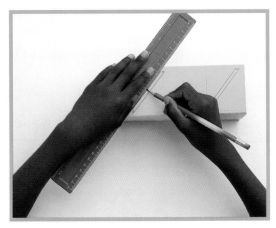

3 Turn the carton over and draw two more right-angled triangles on the opposite side. Make sure that the slots match up with the first slots.

You will need

Colored tape

Shape stickers

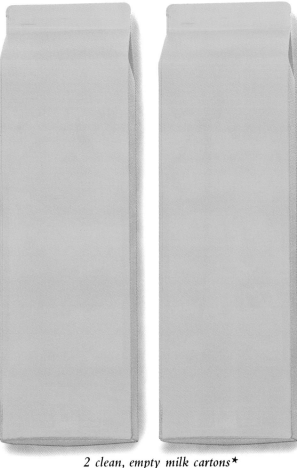

2 clean, empty milk cartons★

2 pocket mirrors
2 x 3 in (5 x 7.5 cm)

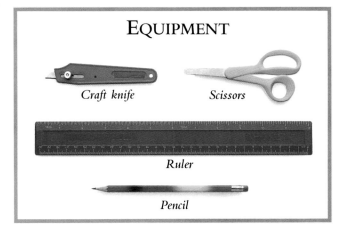

EQUIPMENT

Craft knife

Scissors

Ruler

Pencil

★*To get a smooth surface, paint the cartons before you start.*

4 Slot a pocket mirror facedown through the slots at the top of the carton. Slide the second mirror into the bottom slots, face upward.

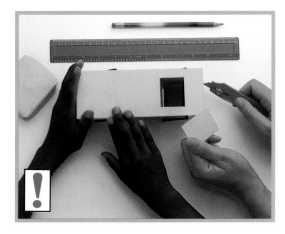

5 Draw a square on the front of the carton over the top mirror. Ask an adult to cut it out. Make a top for the carton from the base of another carton.

6 Cut out a small hole at the back of the carton over the bottom mirror. Then decorate the carton with shape stickers.

Slot the base of the second carton into the periscope to make a new, flat lid. Decorate it in the same way as the rest of the periscope.

Top mirror facing down

Tape the mirror securely in place.

Bottom mirror facing up

Viewing window

Decorated with colorful shapes

Using the periscope

You can use the periscope either by holding it upright, to look over an obstacle, or by turning it sideways, to see around a corner. Close one eye, hold the small hole at the bottom to your open eye, and look through it. What do you see?

Window of periscope must be higher than the obstacle you are looking over.

Reflecting images

A periscope works by reflecting an image from one mirror onto the other. A scene you cannot see over a wall is reflected in the top mirror of the periscope. This is then reflected down onto the bottom mirror. When you look through the small hole at the bottom of the periscope, you see the bottom mirror and the image that is reflected in it.

PAPER POTTERY

Papier-mâché costs very little because it is made out of torn-up newspaper but you can make the most amazing pottery with a few simple molds. Here and on the next page you can see how to create a golden treasure chest and bright plates and bowls for holding and displaying your vacation finds.

For the papier-mâché

Old newspaper and white paper

White glue

You will need

For the treasure chest

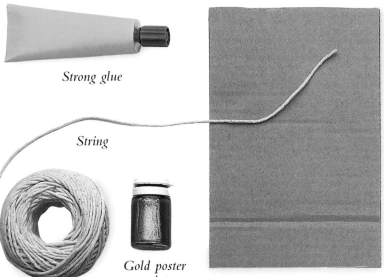

Strong glue

String

Gold poster paint

Corrugated cardboard

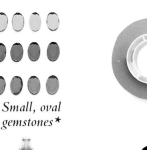

Glitter paint

Small, oval gemstones ★

Large, round gemstones ★

Tape

Box with a lid

Making the plate

1 Tear newspaper into long strips about .75 in (2 cm) across. Mix white glue with a little water in a bowl and soak the paper in it.

2 Using the plate as a mold, cover the back with plastic wrap, then with six layers of glued paper. Make sure all the pieces of paper overlap.

3 Tear up some strips of white paper, soak them in the glue, and cover the plate with them. Leave the papier-mâché to dry for a day.

★*Available from large department or arts and crafts stores.*

EQUIPMENT

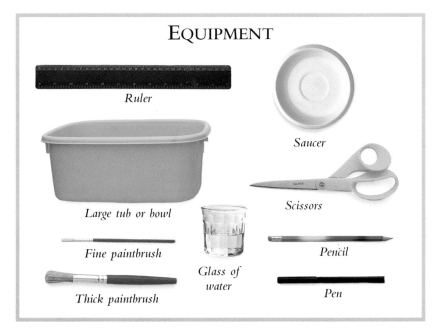

Ruler

Saucer

Large tub or bowl

Scissors

Fine paintbrush

Glass of water

Pencil

Thick paintbrush

Pen

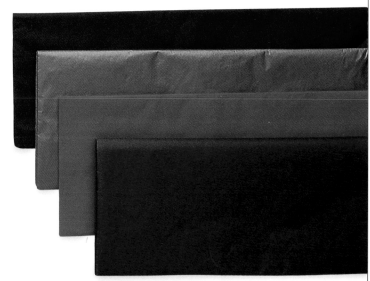

Gold and colored tissue paper

For the plate and bowl

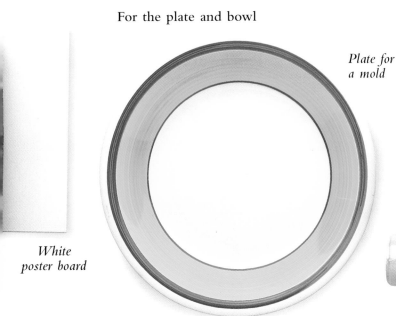

Plate for a mold

White poster board

Poster paints

Large bowl for a mold

Plastic wrap

Decorating the plate

Painting the bowl

4 Remove the mold. Cover the top of the paper plate with white paper soaked in glue. When it is dry, trim the edges of the plate.

Glue squares of colored tissue paper onto the plate. Put gold tissue paper around the rim. Cover the bottom of the plate with gold tissue paper.

Make a bowl in the same way as the plate. Draw a pattern on the bowl, then paint it with poster paint. Paint the inside of the bowl gold.

TREASURE TROVE
Making the chest

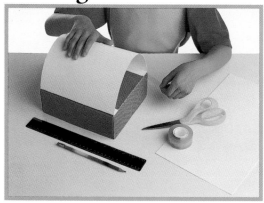

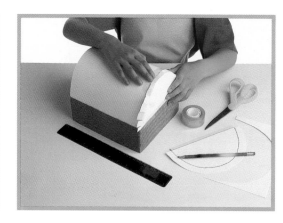

1 Cut out a piece of white poster board the same width as the box lid but twice as long. Fold two flaps and tape them to the top of the lid.

2 Trace around the hole at the side of the lid onto poster board twice. Add .25 in (1 cm) all around and cut out. Fringe the edges and tape in place.

3 Cut a circle and four stars out of corrugated cardboard and glue string on top. Cut a cardboard strip with zigzag edges for the box lid.

Glittering treasures

The finished paper pottery is light, but surprisingly strong. You could use the treasure chest to store interesting bits and pieces. The decorated papier-mâché objects make great presents, too.

Red, blue, and green tissue paper

Foil-covered chocolate coins

Patchwork plate
Squares of brightly colored tissue paper are glued onto the plate to look like patchwork. You could try paler colors, or paint the plate instead.

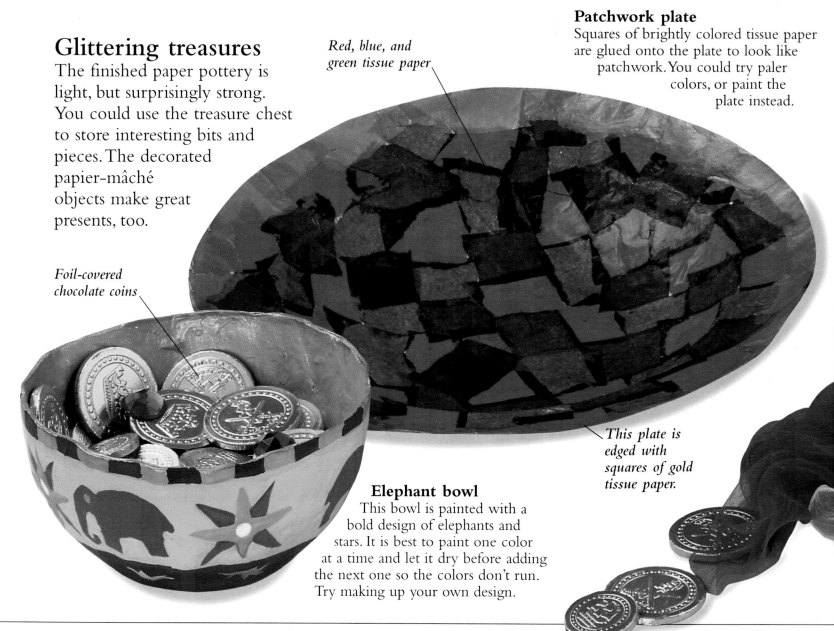

This plate is edged with squares of gold tissue paper.

Elephant bowl
This bowl is painted with a bold design of elephants and stars. It is best to paint one color at a time and let it dry before adding the next one so the colors don't run. Try making up your own design.

4 Cover the box and lid with papier-mâché.★ When dry, glue the zigzag strips to the lid and cover them. Repeat with the shapes.

5 Tear out lots of strips of white paper. Dip them in a mixture of white glue and water and paste them all over the box and lid.

6 When dry, paint the box and lid gold. Then carefully glue oval "jewels" on the box and round ones on the shapes on the box lid.

Star shape made from cardboard and string

Treasure chest
The chunky chest has an old, medieval look. If you can't find "jewels" like those shown here, make your own by covering balls of paper with colored foil candy wrappers.

Oval gemstone

Zigzag edging made from corrugated cardboard

FLOTSAM AND JETSAM

One of the best things about being on vacation by the ocean is looking on the beach for unexpected souvenirs: pieces of sea glass, colored pebbles, unusual shells, and small pieces of twisted driftwood and fishing string. With a little imagination, all this flotsam and jetsam can be transformed into a fun range of natural jewelry and accessories.

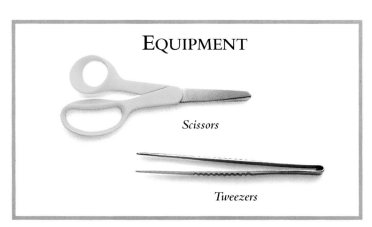

EQUIPMENT

Scissors

Tweezers

You will need

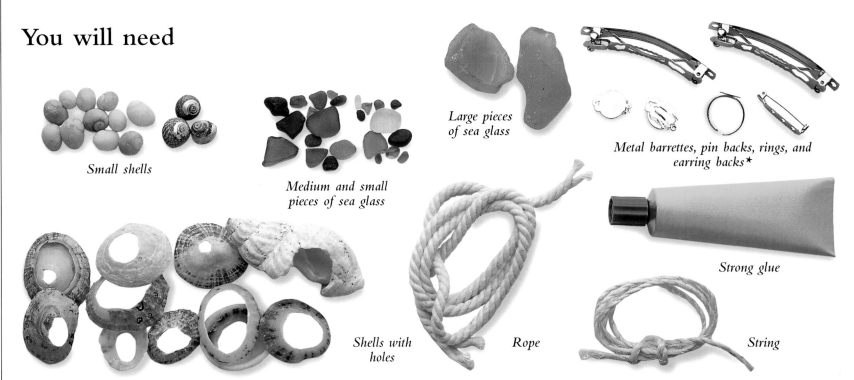

Small shells

Medium and small pieces of sea glass

Large pieces of sea glass

Metal barrettes, pin backs, rings, and earring backs★

Shells with holes

Rope

Strong glue

String

Making the barrettes

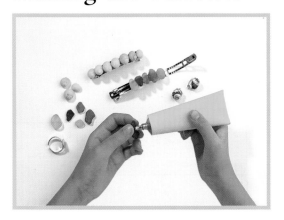

Decorate a barrette by gluing a row of small shells or sea glass along it. Glue single shells or pieces of sea glass onto rings or earring backs.

Making a pin

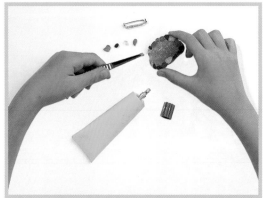

To make a large pin, glue small pieces of sea glass around the edge of a large piece, using tweezers. Glue the big stone to a pin back.

Making a necklace

To make a necklace, thread lots of shells onto a length of rope and knot it. For a key ring, thread a key and shell onto some string and knot it.

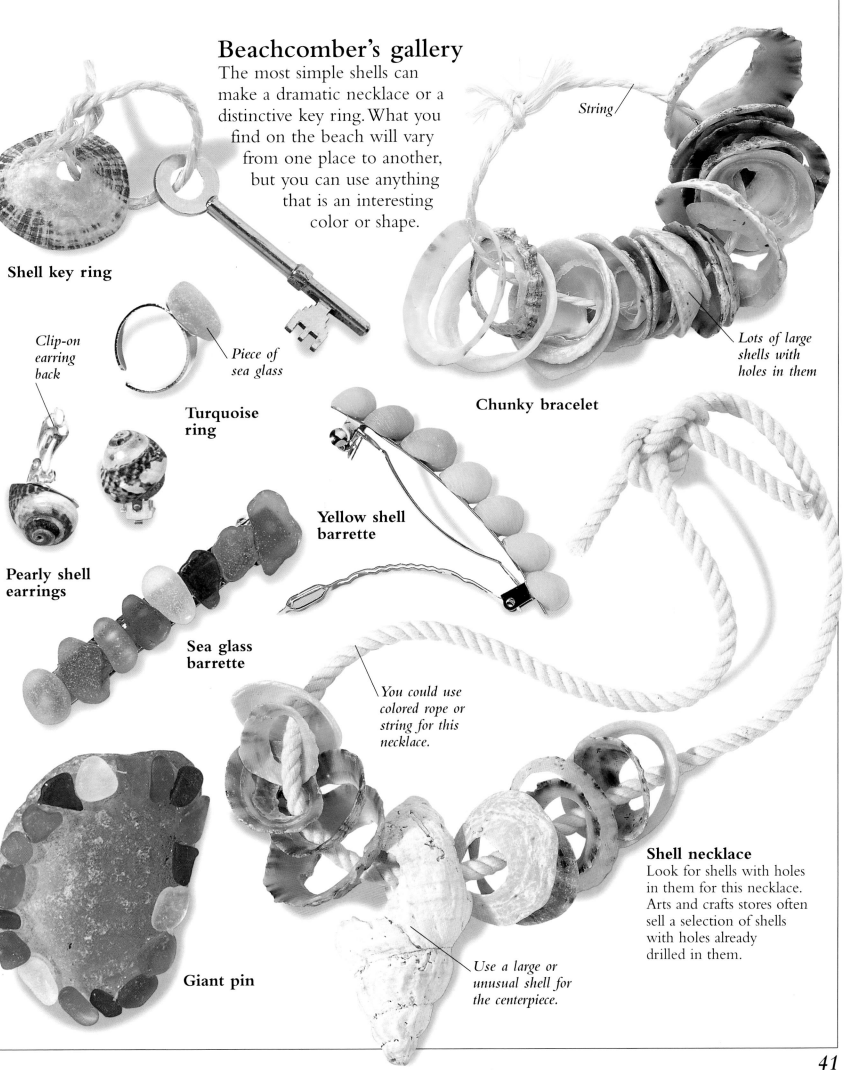

Beachcomber's gallery

The most simple shells can make a dramatic necklace or a distinctive key ring. What you find on the beach will vary from one place to another, but you can use anything that is an interesting color or shape.

Shell key ring

String

Chunky bracelet

Lots of large shells with holes in them

Clip-on earring back

Piece of sea glass

Turquoise ring

Pearly shell earrings

Sea glass barrette

Yellow shell barrette

You could use colored rope or string for this necklace.

Giant pin

Use a large or unusual shell for the centerpiece.

Shell necklace
Look for shells with holes in them for this necklace. Arts and crafts stores often sell a selection of shells with holes already drilled in them.

VACATION SOUVENIRS

Instead of hiding your vacation photos and souvenirs in a box, you can use them to make lasting treasures you'll enjoy all year round. Try creating your own personal travel diary or phrase book, or mount your photographs and give them decorative frames so you can display them in your room.

You will need

For all projects

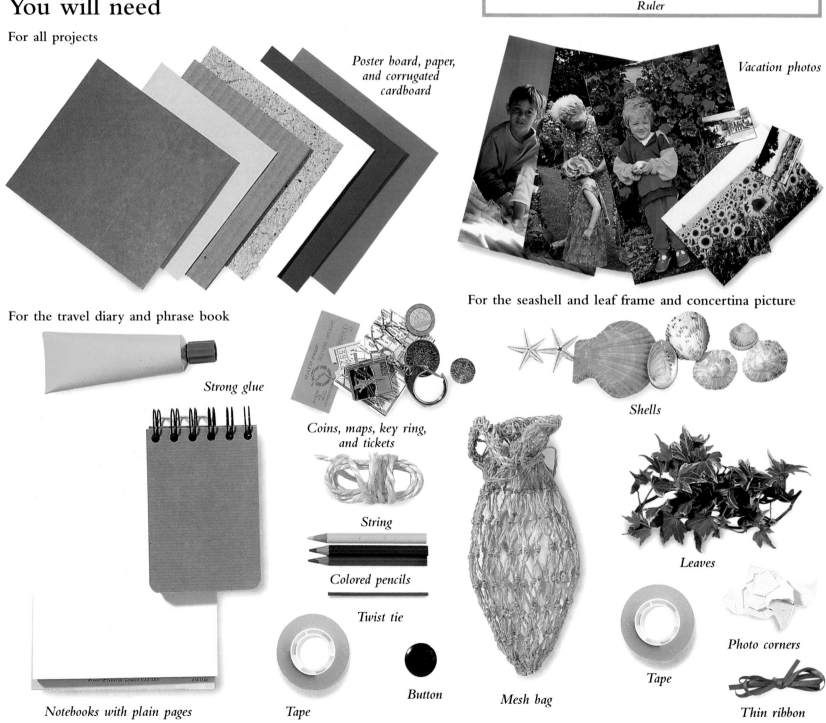

Poster board, paper, and corrugated cardboard

Vacation photos

For the travel diary and phrase book

Strong glue

Coins, maps, key ring, and tickets

For the seashell and leaf frame and concertina picture

Shells

String

Colored pencils

Leaves

Twist tie

Photo corners

Notebooks with plain pages

Tape

Button

Mesh bag

Tape

Thin ribbon

Travel diary

1 For a travel diary cover that looks like the flag of a country you have visited, glue pieces of colored paper to the cover of a notebook.

2 Thread a button onto a twist tie. Make a hole near the edge of the front cover. Thread the tie through it and tape the ends down.

3 Make two small holes in the back cover. Cut some string and thread it through the holes to form a loop. Tie the ends inside the cover.

Seashell frame

1 Cut out a 1-in (3-cm) wide poster board mount, with the center hole just smaller than your photo. Tape the photo to the back of the mount.

2 Cut a 2-in (5-cm) wide frame out of thick cardboard.★ The hole in the middle should be .25 in (1 cm) bigger all around than the mount.

3 Glue textured paper onto the frame to cover it. Glue string mesh on top of this and string around the edge. Decorate with shells on top.

Composite picture

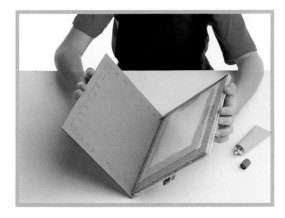

4 Tape the mount to the frame. Cut out some corrugated cardboard the same size as the frame. Glue it to the back of the frame.

1 Cut a rectangle of poster board with four equal rectangular holes. Trim the photos and tape them, face-up, to the back of the mount.

2 Glue the mount to a thick piece of cardboard. Make a frame bigger than the mount and tape it to the corners of the mount.

★*You can make the frame as wide as you like, to look right with your picture.*

WORDS AND PICTURES

Concertina picture

1 For four 4 x 6 in (10 x 15 cm) photos, cut out a piece of poster board 7.5 x 22 in (19 x 56 cm). Score a vertical line every 5.5 in (14 cm).

2 Cut a slot at each side. Tie and knot ribbons through the slots. Slip photo corners on the photos and glue the corners down.

Vacation memories

The pictures and notebooks bring back memories of many different vacations – by the ocean, at home, or visiting a foreign country. You can adapt any of these ideas to suit your own particular vacation.

Red poster board

Frame decorated with leaves

Concertina vacation picture
When you have finished, stand the concertina picture on a desk or shelf. To give it as a present, tie the ends of the ribbon together to keep it flat.

Composite vacation picture
Close-up photos work well with this mount. Decorate the frame with leaves, bark, or twigs.

Ribbon tied to slot

Photo corner

Seashell frame
This sandy looking seashell frame reflects the theme of the two girls on the beach.

Poster board mount

String border

Textured paper

Shell

Netting glued to the paper

Phrase book
Use a small, spiral-bound notebook to create your own phrase book. Draw small pictures of everyday things, then write down the foreign words or phrases for them next to the pictures.

Le pain

La confiture

Le fromage

Les tomates

La bouteille d'eau

French words

Button fastening

Loop of string

Colored paper

Travel diary cover
This cover looks like the French flag. It has been covered with rectangles of blue, white, and red paper.

Eiffel Tower

My French souvenirs

METROPOLITAIN

CHATEAU DE CHENONCEAU
Propriété Privée
Entrée pour
1 personne
392776

Map

Coin

Ticket

Vacation souvenirs
You can glue all kinds of different souvenirs into your travel diary: here French coins, maps, photos, postcards, and tickets are displayed.

Photo

POSTCARDS HOME

Making your own postcards is lots of fun and your friends and family will treasure the cards as vacation memories. Choose a theme based on where you are spending your vacation – by the sea, in the country, or in a city – and remember to write an interesting message on the back.

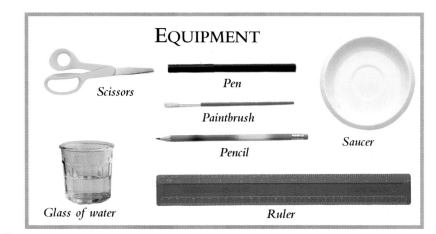

EQUIPMENT

Scissors

Pen

Paintbrush

Pencil

Saucer

Glass of water

Ruler

You will need

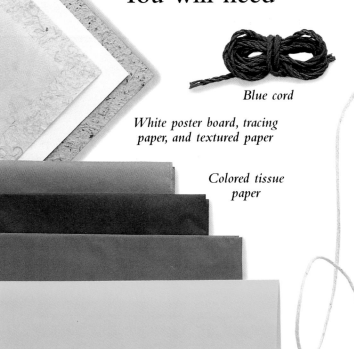

White poster board, tracing paper, and textured paper

Colored tissue paper

Blue cord

Glue stick

Small seashells

String

Strong glue

Poster paints

Making a postcard

1 Measure and cut out pieces of poster board the size you want your postcards. Carefully draw and then paint different pictures on them.

2 If you want to make a collage, cut out one of your paintings. Make a background on another card by gluing on torn pieces of paper.

3 Glue the painting to the background card. Carefully add any final details. Leave the back of the card blank to write your message on.

Postcard gallery

All these cards have a seaside theme. Some are simply painted, some have cutout shapes, and others are collages with different things stuck on them. If you are worried about a special postcard being damaged in the mail, make an envelope for it out of thick paper or send it in a small box.

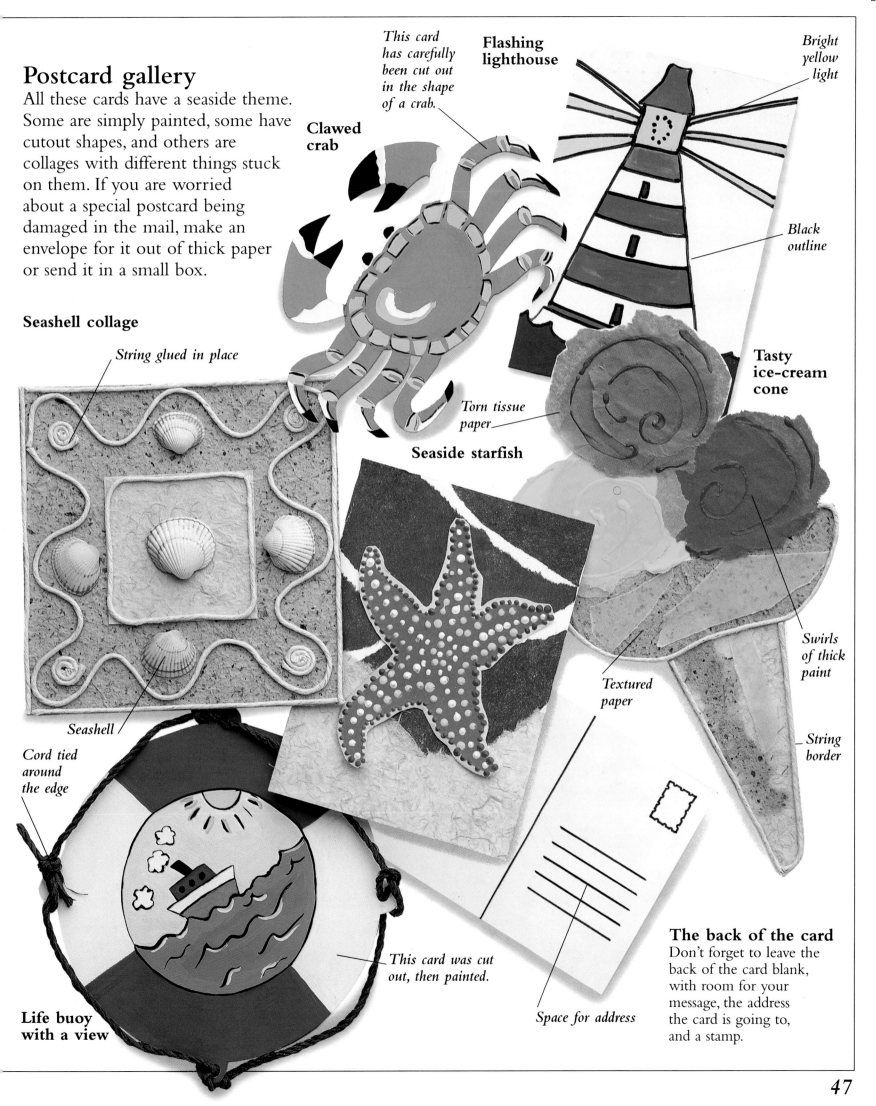

This card has carefully been cut out in the shape of a crab.

Clawed crab

Flashing lighthouse

Bright yellow light

Black outline

Seashell collage

String glued in place

Tasty ice-cream cone

Torn tissue paper

Seaside starfish

Seashell

Swirls of thick paint

Cord tied around the edge

Textured paper

String border

Life buoy with a view

This card was cut out, then painted.

Space for address

The back of the card
Don't forget to leave the back of the card blank, with room for your message, the address the card is going to, and a stamp.

INDEX